# DEXTER CHASE
## Gay Erotica

# THE
# LOSER
# BOYFRIEND MANDATE

## WARNING

This book contains sexually explicit scenes and adult language. It may be considered offensive to some readers. This book is for sale to adults ONLY.

\* \* \* \* \* \* \* \* \* \* \* \* \* \* \* \* \* \* \*

Please store your files wisely where they cannot be accessed by underage readers.

Please feel free to send me an email. Just know that these emails are filtered by my publisher. Good news is always welcome.

Dexter Chase - **dexter_chase@awesomeauthors.org**

**About the Publisher**

**4Fun Publishing,** a member of **BLVNP Incorporated**, 340 S. Lemon #6200, Walnut CA 91789, info@blvnp.com / legal@blvnp.com
NOTE: Due to the highly emotional reaction of some people to works of erotic fiction, any email sent to the above address that contains foul language or religious references is automatically deleted by our anti-spam software and will not be seen. All other communications are welcome.

**DISCLAIMER**

Please don't be stupid and kill yourself. This book is a work of FICTION. Do not try any new sexual practice that you find in this book. It is fiction and not to be confused with reality. Neither the author nor the publisher or its associates assume any responsibility for any loss, injury, death or legal consequences resulting from acting on the contents in this book. Every character in this book is over 18 years of age. The author's opinions are not to be construed as the opinions of the publisher. The material in this book is for entertainment purposes ONLY. Enjoy.

# The Loser

*Boyfriend Mandate*

## Gay Erotica

By: Dexter Chase

© **Dexter Chase 2014**
ISBN: 978-1-68030-140-3

# Part 1

The drive seemed to take forever. It was so uncomfortable that after a few hours Gary was close to tears. The truck looked comfortable enough in the front section, but the covered rear portion was very cold with basic plastic seats. The wrist cuffs were clipped to his belt and the ankle chains were secured to the floor of the truck. Movement was very restricted and the cold had slowly seeped into his body until he was almost freezing.

"You have been found guilty of multiple robberies and are sentenced to five years hard labour."

That was the start of the nightmare. Gary had been up in court so many times it was laughable and he thought this would be just another appearance to have his wrist slapped and then he would be back on the street. The jails were all overflowing so where was he going to do his five years?

"His Honour has sanctioned you being attached to a chain gang on the estate of his friend the Marquis of Kilkenny."

That didn't sound like anything he wanted to hear and everything went downhill from there. First he was stripped and then clothed in just a coverall, no socks and only a pair of canvas shoes. The wrist and ankle cuffs were fitted and a chain was put round his waist to link to the wrist cuffs. The chain joining the ankle cuffs was only about a foot long so all he could do was shuffle. The final object to attach to him was a metal collar.

"The collar contains a GPS tracking device so if you try to run away they'll catch you in no time, and then you'll know real pain because the law decrees a public whipping for escapees."

He had been loaded into the truck with a driver and guard, but whereas they sat in heated comfort in the front, he was in the canvas-covered rear with no heat. It couldn't have been a worse month to be in this situation. February and there was snow over almost the whole of the British Isles.

On the way North, Gary had time to reflect on his life. He had joined the army after leaving school but that had not worked out. He was small for his age and despite a gym trained body he took so much grief over his size that he beat up on an NCO, (non- commissioned officer), who took the Mickey one too many times. Court Martial and a dishonourable discharge followed. Back to civilian life and still only nineteen, no one wanted a rebel who had been dismissed by his regiment, so a life of crime followed to survive. Parents dead and no siblings, his life became an empty shell emotionally. He lived from hand to mouth and in some ways was glad he would be looked after now, and hard work didn't worry him, but somewhere in the desolate wastes of Scotland, as he saw it, was not his idea of fun.

He lost interest in the scenery, what he could see of it, because it was all white. He could hear the sound of the tires scrunching on the hard snow and if he hadn't been so cold he would probably have slept, but the further north they went the colder he became. The change in the road noise eventually made him come alive and look at where they were going. The truck had turned off the main road and was now on a clear tarmacadam road that was only wide enough for the truck, but with passing places every few hundred yards. The road was well made and smooth, either side was mature trees and neat fences. The fields were all snow covered so the contrast was dramatic. The black road appeared to go on for miles until they pulled up in front of an incredible castle like structure. It was patently very old, but perfectly maintained. He could barely stand when he was pulled from his seat onto the gravel drive, just as the front door opened and a colossus of a man dressed in a kilt stood, hands on hips and thunder in his eyes.

"What are ye doing bringing trash to the front of the house?"

The driver looked quite intimidated and spluttered out that he didn't know any other entrance.

"Well, we'd better get him inside and hope his Lordship does ne see him."

Papers were signed and the driver and guard disappeared. This took long enough for Gary to look at his surroundings. The entrance door was quite small, but the entrance hall was magnificent. Four large pillars supported the high ceiling and it was about thirty feet square, Gary guessed. There were large sofas and coffee tables spread out on a deep pile carpet with display cabinets on the walls. On one wall was a fireplace, almost big enough to walk into and burning warmly in the grate were large logs pumping out the heat that Gary needed. Ahead of him was a magnificent staircase rising up from beyond an arch. To his right he could see through a partly open door that there was a huge library with French doors leading out onto a lawn. While he was waiting, the door opened fully and a young man filled it, dressed casually in beige cavalry trousers with an open necked shirt.

"What's going on here, Hamish?"

"I'm sorry your Lordship, the prisoner transport brought the new boy to the front door. I'll take him away immediately."

The man gave Gary the once over, noting his small size.

Gary meanwhile had done likewise. The Marquis was mid-twenties he guessed. A handsome man with aristocratic features, as one would expect. His voice although carrying a Scottish accent was quite soft, but carried a commanding tone. *'So this is my new boss'* was Gary's thought.

"He looks half frozen to death Hamish. You'd better take him to the staff quarters and put him under a hot shower, bring him back to me when he is warm and cleaned up. Take those awful chains and restraints off him as well."

With that the Marquis turned back into the library.

"Tell him the rules as well Hamish," came wafting back to him as he was led through the house to a bathroom in the servant's quarters.

"Make the most of this shower, boy. The labour gangs only have cold water in their quarters."

Gary thought that was monstrous. He thought life was going to be more than a little miserable here. On the way through the house he was also shown the labour gangs' quarters. They were four man cells, with no heating, he was informed these were the old dungeons, and they looked it. *'Oh God, what have I been sent to?'* was his dejected thought. The hot shower though, in the staff quarters, was marvellous, he could feel the heat seeping back into his frozen body. Hamish talked as he soaked.

"Now, listen carefully boy. If his Lordship wants you to know the rules he must be thinking about having you in the house. Considerably better than working in the fields and barns at this time of year. The house is heated throughout so the prisoners that work in the house work almost naked unless we have guests. The rules that ensure your employment in the house are easy. Whatever you are asked to do, you do it without hesitation. That means anything. If the Marquis tells you to strip so that he can look at you, you strip without hesitation. If he tells you to stand still while he feels your body, you stand still. He won't tell you twice, one slip up and you'll be working in the fields ten hours a day and believe me it isn't pleasant at this time of year. The men live in a permanent state of cold."

Gary determined to remain in the house to work. He wasn't a wimp, but he did like being warm. Now thoroughly warm, he was given another set of coveralls, but these were good quality and fitted him properly. The shoes were canvas again but of better quality and quite comfortable.

"Follow me lad and remember what I have told you. His Lordship doesn't like staff to use long titles so just address him as Sir, when you speak. You only speak when spoken to and then only yes or no sir. He likes you to stand straight and proud and look him in the eyes when you speak or are spoken to.

*'Christ, it's like being back in the army'*, Gary thought.

Taken back to the library, Gary was told to stand in the bay window, his back to the French doors. Hamish knocked on a panel at the side of the open fireplace currently pumping out a huge amount of heat from the logs burning in the hearth. The panel opened and the Marquis stepped through. He faced Gary and said, "Well, boy we'd better have a look at you to see if you'll fit in here. Your record isn't very good though is it?"

Gary looked him in the eyes, remembered Hamish's words and replied.

"No Sir."

"Would you like to work indoors if we can train you properly?"

"Oh, yes Sir." That came out very enthusiastically, making the Marquis smile.

"In that case, get rid of your coveralls, let me have a look at you."

Gary nearly blew it then, he was going to say he was naked underneath, but then he realised his Lordship would know that. He quickly undid the buttons, slid them off his shoulders, stooped to pick them up and fold them before putting them on a chair and returning to stand to attention in front of his boss. He knew he was blushing but his mind was on that indoor job.

The Marquis just looked at him for ages and so did Hamish. The picture was very pleasant. Gary had a straightforward appearance, his eyes were honest, David, the Marquis, wondered why he had turned to crime when his eyes denied he would do that. The body was lightly muscled, but all of the groups looked well formed. He was a good colour all over indicating that he probably sun tanned naked, the tan didn't look as though it had been obtained on a tanning bed. The hair was mid brown and tousled which David found enchanting. The groin looked interesting and David moved in to stroke Gary's body, moving quickly to the groin area. Gary didn't move, but never took his eyes off his lordship. The penis came to full erection and David gasped. It was beautiful, about seven inches long and quite thick, circumcised with a good size and shape to the glans.

"Turn round boy and let's have a look at the back view."

"Open your legs wide." Gary did.

One look was enough for David, the arse was perfect. He was erect thinking about sliding his cock into this gorgeous creature. His uncle had done him a great favour he thought, sending him this boy. He slid his hand over the back and shoulders before stroking the cheeks and sliding a finger down the crack to touch the rosebud. Gary didn't move but he was blushing furiously, knowing that Hamish was watching all this as well. He started to sweat when he felt David's fingers touch his anus, but he still didn't move. *'He can fuck me and I still won't protest or move, as long as I can work in the house',* was Gary's thought.

Inspection complete, David told Gary to stand and face him again.

"Hamish, I'm going to take the boy through to the office. Come back for him in half an hour will you?"

"Yes Sir, of course."

Hamish went, Gary followed David through the panel in the wall to an office with a desk, chair and filing cabinets. Two armchairs were in front of the desk, but the rest of the room was patently a business area.

"Sit down Gary and relax."

Gary sat, but he didn't relax. What did this strange man want from him? The feeling was that David was gay and wanted his body, if that was the case he would go with the flow. He didn't know if he could accept a gay relationship, he had never given it a moment's thought. Girls had always found him attractive so he had taken the easy route and gone with them.

"I have no female staff Gary, so, I would like you to train as a valet and housekeeper. Do you think you would like that?"

*'Be honest if you don't want to blow this'*, Gary thought.

"I had to look after my uniforms in the army, Sir, so I guess looking after you wouldn't be too difficult, and learning to keep your home clean and tidy shouldn't stretch my ability."

David laughed.

"Well said boy. Now for the big one. I think I would like to take you for my lover. How do you feel about that?"

Gary became quite flustered, he hadn't expected David to be this blunt even though he had the idea he might be used sexually.

"I don't know, Sir, I have never had sex with another male. I don't have any problem with it in principle but I don't know whether I would enjoy it and make you enjoy it with me."

David was pleased with the answer.

"I'll do a deal with you then. You come to bed with me until one of us decides it isn't working satisfactorily and we will call it quits. I'll still employ you in the house provided you measure up."

Gary smiled a shy smile at this attractive but strange man.

"I'm going to give you to Hamish, he'll get the other house staff to teach you what you need to know, and I'll teach you what you need to know to enjoy our sex, first lesson now. I'm going to give you a blowjob. I can't wait any longer to get my lips around that gorgeous cock."

Gary was almost in shock as David dropped to his knees in front of him and took his cock into his mouth. The shock turned to pleasure as he received a blow job to beat anything he had ever experienced in sexual arousal. When he orgasmed he almost passed out, it was so intense.

"Judging by the volume of your love juice, I presume you enjoyed that?"

Gary almost gushed, "Oh yes Sir that was amazing."

David was grinning as he returned to his seat.

"Do you think you could do that to me with a little training?"

"I would certainly try very hard, Sir."

"Good, I will tell Hamish to put you in the valet's room and to start your domestic training in the morning. You had better remain in coveralls for now and I'll get my tailor to come and measure you for your other clothes. I'm sure we will have dress shorts available so when appropriate you can wear them and the estate polo shirt. Off you go now, get dressed again and wait for Hamish."

Gary was reeling when he eventually got himself together. Had this last half an hour been for real? Was he really going to be the lover of the Marquis?

When Hamish returned he went straight into the office. Gary could hear the conversation but not make out the individual words. When the door opened again Hamish looked at him and said, "You must be a very special boy, come with me."

Gary happily trotted along behind Hamish as they climbed the staircase to the next floor, and then another one. He was shown into a bedroom that was about twice as big as the one he had grown up with. He thought it was David's and was overwhelmed when Hamish told him.

"This is your bedroom. The bathroom is through that door. His Lordship's suite is through that door," pointing to another door, "Come, we might as well look at it."

Gary's jaw dropped as he saw the master suite. David's bed was huge but was dwarfed by the remainder of the room. There was a large sitting area almost as big as that in the library with sofas and coffee tables, a dining table and chairs suitable for up to four people and doors leading off to bathroom and dressing room. There was a huge bay window that had banquette seating all round it, looking across the lawns and gardens to a covered swimming pool and. There was also a large fireplace on one wall, and like the others he had seen around the house, it was lit and pumping out more heat than Gary would have been happy sleeping with.

"Why does his Lordship have these fires in every room when I can see the heating vents in the floor?"

"Because he loves open fires and the estate always has trees that need cutting so he makes good use of the wood."

Gary had never seen real wealth in play and realised he loved it, even living as a servant in this house would be an amazing experience.

"If you make the grade I expect you will have to look after this, but his Lordship has a member of staff responsible for the fires, I don't suppose you will have to do anything more than feed it in this room."

Back in his own room Hamish completed his briefing.

"If you turn right outside your room you will come to the staff staircase, go down it, turn left and that will take you to the staff dining room. Until seven you can wander round the house to familiarise yourself with it."

With that, he was gone and Gary sat down on his bed, almost in shock. Christ, if this was hard labour he would be happy to do it for ten years, never mind five. He was a little worried about the sex side because he had heard that gay men fucked and he wasn't sure about that. He looked round his bedroom, pushed his nose into his bathroom, and then thought, 'I'm going to make a big effort to like whatever the Marquis likes.'

# Part 2

Gary was about to start his voyage of discovery when there was a knock on his door. The body that greeted him when he opened it just handed him a watch and told him Mr. Hamish had said to deliver it. *'No excuse to be late for dinner now'*, Gary thought as he slipped the watch over his wrist. He asked the delivery boy who he was.

"I'm Archer."

Gary put out his hand and said, "I'm Gary, pleased to meet you."

Archer looked at it, looked at Gary and slowly put his own hand out as he said, "You're going to be his lordship's fancy boy then."

Gary blushed. "I think so, he said I had the choice, the fields or here. I didn't think I would like the fields when it's cold. I just hope I can give his lordship what he wants."

"You're not queer then?"

Gary didn't like the way this conversation was going.

"I don't know, I've never done anything with a boy before."

Archer laughed then and slung an arm round Gary pulling him gently into a hug.

"We'll try to look after you then. The Marquis goes through lovers quite rapidly. He always appears to pick straight boys who eventually decide the fields are a better bet than his lordship's bed. Come on, I'll show you round the house, I have nothing to do for about half an hour."

The guided tour was very revealing. The staff quarters were quite extensive with the dungeon being the centre of occupancy. House staff had similar accommodation but it was heated and their bathroom had hot water. The remainder of the house had two large dining rooms, one was the formal one for large banquets and the other was smaller and just for the house occupants. There were three lounges referred to by their colour and two of them had grand pianos in them. Everywhere was deep carpeted and looked very luxurious.

"There are three full time houseboys who do nothing but clean. One more who does everything to do with linen and there are three in the kitchen including the chef. You will have to look after your room and the Marquis's I expect but Tommy will see to the laundry if you give it to him. We are all criminals doing hard labour, sent by the same judge. The Marquis has no labour costs except Hamish, the head Groom and the Estate Manager. Pretty neat set up for him don't you think?"

Gary nodded.

"Can you ride a horse Gary?"

Shake of the head so Archer told him. "You will do, his Lordship rides almost every day, he'll want you to accompany him if you're his fancy piece."

Gary didn't like being called that but thought he would probably have to get used to it.

"What do you do here Archer?"

"I'm one of the houseboys. I tried your job for a little while, but I didn't like getting fucked. His Lordship let me stay on in the house though."

Gary thought, wow, this is some weird setup.

"You might get the chance to fuck him instead of the other way round. If you do I bet you'll enjoy it. Fucking arse is a bit special."

Almost overload again, Gary had never thought about sodomy before, now he had to contemplate doing it as well as receiving it.

By the time they finished the guided tour, Gary had come to like Archer. He was easy going and like Gary had been convicted for persistent burglary.

"I didn't like work so burglary was the easiest way to make money. None of us here have convictions for violence, just for stupidity I guess."

"Yeah, like me, never thought I'd get sent down."

Gary met the remainder of the prisoners at dinner. The field hands were easy to place, they all looked cold and tended to sit nearest the heating vents, also, as everybody else left they hung on and Archer told him they stayed in the dining room until Hamish threw them out.

"Breakfast for you at seven Gary and then find Archer, he'll be teaching you tomorrow."

Gary liked that but now worried about getting up on time.

"Don't worry Gary, I'll call you on your room phone."

"Thanks Archer, I guess I'm going to need an alarm clock or I'll be in trouble."

"I doubt it, you'll soon be sleeping with his lordship every night so you won't need anything like that."

Another piece of information for Gary to digest.

The next morning went as planned, Gary started to learn the house method for cleaning everything and Archer made it fun. Lunch time and Gary knew he was going to make it as the fancy boy. He just had to take one look at the field hands. They looked one stage short of hypothermia. The afternoon went very much the same as the morning, only most of the work took place in his lordship's suite. Gary noticed that everything had to be left immaculate. Loose clothing was checked to see if it needed cleaning, if not it was put away in the dressing room. Boots and shoes were all checked and where necessary cleaned.

"The cleaning kit is in your room Gary with a pile of old newspapers so that none of the polish goes on the carpet."

The clothing and footwear was no problem for Gary, he had done similar with his own uniforms always being very smart on parade.

Hamish caught him as he and Archer were leaving the dining room after tea.

"His lordship wants to see you in his suite Gary. Go straight up."

Archer whispered, "First lesson, you'll be taught how to suck."

Gary winced, and hoped he would like it.

He knocked lightly on the main door to David's suite and heard the 'come in', muffled by the thickness of the door. When he entered, he saw David curled up on a sofa in front of the fire reading. He was wearing a dressing gown so Gary guessed what was going to happen shortly.

"Come in Gary, sit here with me."

The room was softly lit with table lamps. It looked very romantic with the logs burning and crackling in the fireplace and the flames reflecting off the furniture.

"I thought we ought to get to know each other a little better if we are going to be lovers. Feel free to ask me any questions you like."

In very quick time Gary found out that David was 26 years old, had a degree from St. Andrews University and had become the 14th Marquis of Kilkenny on the death of his parents the previous year. He was an only child and gay, so Gary immediately wanted to know what would happen to the title and the estate when he died.

"Ah, I've got that covered already. A well-bred young lady is currently carrying the heir to my title. A surrogate mother of impeccable character, also a graduate of St. Andrews, will eventually move in to the gate house on the estate and raise my son."

Gary grinned as his thought turned into a word, "Crafty."

David grinned as well.

"Do you like children Gary?"

"Mmm, I'm not sure, I've never really had anything to do with them apart from when I was one myself."

"Well, if you and I make it through the next few years you might be part of the growing up experience of my son."

That was a surprise.

"I don't want to sound impertinent Sir, but don't you change lovers quite frequently?"

David looked at Gary and then smiled before replying.

"Yes I do, because I haven't found the lover I want to be long term. I hope that will change with you. I like a lot of sex, and sometimes I will want it with more than one person, but most of all I want a companion and friend that I can do lots of things with. I know you don't have a degree but I have your educational stats and I see you are quite clever and intelligent. You just need steering in the right direction to be a good citizen. I'll give you that chance if you let me mould you. We'll ride, swim, work out, and indulge our taste buds, frequently away from the estate. When you are a free man again we'll start travelling as well. I'll think long term with you and see how it works. I suppose I'm a bit shallow in that your looks and sex appeal were the first things I noticed and sucking your penis yesterday was wonderful. You have a very sexy body and a gorgeous penis."

Gary was blushing furiously, but began to laugh when David did, and kept it up even when David pulled him into a hug and kissed him on the nose.

"Let's go to bed for a little while Gary and start your sex lesson, just a short session this evening to see how you like it."

Gary looked apprehensive until David stroked his cheek to gain his attention.

"I'm not going to embarrass you, or force the pace. I'll get naked first and then you can let me undress you."

Sense of humour to the fore Gary replied, "That won't take long Sir, I only have my coveralls on the same as yesterday."

They both laughed as David stood up and dropped his robe. Gary gasped, he was looking at a reasonably well put together man just seven years older than him. He was already sporting a hard penis that made Gary gulp. David saw where the eyes were and spoke again.

"I promise I won't hurt you with it even when I feed it into your bottom."

Gary was looking at about seven or eight inches of an uncut cock, reasonable thickness with two low hanging balls behind it. He noted that the abs could do with some work and his lordship needed to do a little nude sun bathing to make the colour below the waist sexier.

Whoops, what was he doing making those observations?

A minute later and he was facing David, also naked, and soon after, sporting an erection. David's hands were very soft and the stroking of cock and balls was very erotic.

"I want to enjoy your cock again Gary so we'll 69 and I'll teach you how to pleasure me by example. Have you showered this evening?"

"Yes Sir, before tea."

"Good, let's give this a try. It might be a little clinical until we see if you are enjoying man on man sex. Also Gary, please call me David whenever we are alone."

For Gary, that last statement sounded like a serious commitment.

*'If I perform well and enjoy this, I think David may become someone special in my life.'* That thought was what made this first session so successful, Gary genuinely wanted to please this strange man and was lucky, the sex was good.

"Everything I do to you, you try to do with me, Ok?"

Gary grinned and said, "Ok."

Taking hold of Gary's hard penis, David pulled it away from his body and started to lick the glans and worry the piss slit. Gary did the same. Very tentative to start with but when he realised it tasted ok, he showed more enthusiasm making David gasp. Licking moved to sucking and playing with the balls. That moved to pressure stroking the perineum and gently worrying the anus. The sucking and ball play became more intense until David had a mighty orgasm, filling Gary's mouth with copious amounts of cum. Not knowing what else to do, Gary swallowed it and was pleased it tasted quite sweet. He came then doing the same as he had before with David. Calming down, David swivelled round and kissed Gary on the lips.

"That was very special Boy, did you enjoy that?"

Gary was still only partly with it when he replied, but his words carried conviction, "Oh yes David, that was incredible."

They cuddled for a little while before David slid out of bed and put his robe back on.

"There is a robe in your wardrobe Gary, why don't you go and put it on before returning here?"

Gary scooped up his coveralls and went through to his own bedroom. The robe he found in his wardrobe was silk and felt wonderful on his body.

Back with David and a brandy snifter was presented to him.

"This is a fine old cognac. Sip it and tell me if you could get used to it."

They sat on the sofa again and Gary took a sip. It was like silk, but with a bite to it. It lit a fire in his stomach that made him glow.

"Oh yes, David, I will have no trouble making friends with this."

David laughed. "I'm so pleased, it is very civilised to go to bed with the glow of cognac inside you. Will you sleep with me tonight?"

Gary nodded and wondered if his sex education would continue in bed.

It was still quite early, but Gary went off to clean his teeth before sliding into bed with David, both quite naked. They lay together talking for a little while before David turned out all the lights from a single switch by his bedside. He pulled Gary into a cuddle and before he knew it, both of them were asleep.

Because they had gone to bed quite early it was also early when they woke up.

"Let's shower together and then we'll raid the kitchen for an early breakfast. I have to go into Edinburgh today for business and Archer will continue teaching you your duties until the tailor arrives. I've told him what I require for you so that we can start doing things outside."

Gary shuddered, the ice and snow outside the windows reminded him of how cold it was there.

"Don't worry little one, we'll wrap you up as warm as a bug in a rug."

Gary laughed and relaxed. They showered and shaved together. Gary looked at David quizzically after the shower having expected a little sex play at least. David laughed having read Gary's thoughts.

"We probably will some mornings, but I want to take things slowly with you until you are sure this is what you want."

Gary glowed seeing how David was being considerate.

"Thank you David, I am really enjoying being with you so far. I like blowjobs, giving and receiving and I hope I get good for you. I'm just a little worried about the anal thing though."

David stroked Gary's face and spoke quite softly.

"I know, we'll just have to hope you enjoy it. For me it is a very important part of love making."

Gary nodded, slipped on his coverall and was ready to go. He watched David dress, casually for now.

Breakfast was fun. No one else was about so they played house like a couple of kids, making a mess but ending up with a half presentable breakfast.

"Mmm, I don't think we'll do this too often Gary, cook does a much better job than us."

Both were giggling like schoolgirls when cook walked in ready to start his day.

"Oh, good morning Sir, you should have called me to get your breakfast."

"Not to worry Cook, Gary and I had fun, I'm sorry we made so much mess."

Back in David's suite they were still giggling when Archer knocked on Gary's door.

"Off you go Gary, Hamish will call you when the tailor arrives."

A gentle kiss on the lips, which Gary realised he liked and he was off for his second day of instruction.

"Ok Sport, what was your first night like, I can see you didn't sleep in your own bed."

"No, I slept with David and it was fine. I like him, he's very gentle and considerate."

"Aye, he's all that, he was with me as well. I just wasn't into all the anal sex, he really does like to fuck and occasionally to be fucked. If you enjoy it, life will be good for you here. I still have a smashing wardrobe to take with me when I leave here and David promised to get me settled in to a flat and help me find a job. He's a good man for all his sexuality. Our agreement means you may end up fucking me when he has his little orgies. I agreed to a few sex sessions as part of my guaranteed living in the house."

He scoped Archer out, thinking he was a very cute guy so sex with him would probably be good as well if the anal business worked ok. He still worried about it. An army doctor had checked his prostate when he had joined up, but apart from that he had never had anything in his arse. He tried to remember what it felt like, but it was such a brief intrusion more than a year ago so the memory was fuzzy.

The tailor, when he arrived, was old but very efficient. Gary was quite surprised to be told to remove his coveralls.

"But I don't have anything on underneath."

"If you had I would have told you to remove that as well. The Marquis wants you clothed from the skin out and from the toes up."

He produced a pack of briefs. "Try a pair of these. They are the style the Marquis likes and he told me your build so I'm guessing these will fit."

They were Hom mini briefs, brilliant white and they fitted perfectly.

"Good, you may keep them on."

He then proceeded to measure everywhere.

"I would like you to get an erection so that I can see where we will fit it within tight trousers like your riding breeches."

Gary was shocked, and struggled to get an erection with the old man watching. He had to dress it to the side when he was hard because it would pop out of the top of his briefs otherwise.

"That is very impressive young man, I shall have to remember that when I cut your pants."

Gary was quite tickled by this comment and grinned. The tailor grinned back and just touched the swollen member.

"Ah that I were thirty years younger."

Gary relaxed now, this man was so easy to like.

"I haven't done very much on the sex front with men, but if you would like to do anything I don't think I would mind, but you would have to keep it a secret from David because he might get upset."

"Ah, David is wiser than you think. He knows this is a voyage of discovery for you. He told me I could play if you were willing."

With that the tailor peeled Gary's briefs off, dropped to his knees and gave him another blowjob. Gary loved it, all this gay sex was very exciting. He so hoped he would feel the same with a cock in his bottom.

Back to work, now wearing underpants, Gary was in fine mood, picked up on by Archer.

"The tailor isn't as exciting as David, but he's not bad is he?"

Gary laughed, "No he's pretty good and I suppose the same thing happened to you."

Archer giggled, "Yes, a blowjob after all the measuring, and a nice set of mini briefs."

Gary knew then that he could quiz Archer to find out what would happen next and how it would all progress.

"It will be different for you if you like butt fucking, I had a long period of trying to like it and our relationship got worse until I bowed out. I'm sure if you enjoy it your future training will be very different. I expect you'll find out tonight. David is an impatient lover to get where he wants to be. My guess is that tomorrow morning you will know if you are going to join me or remain in your own suite, well David's more often than your own."

Both boys laughed, but Gary was very apprehensive.

After dinner that night the action started. David took Gary to his suite and they showered together, but not until Gary had been given three douches. David made light of it so the nozzle in his arse had been turned into a joke, as had the pregnant look when he was full. They pampered each other in the shower, Gary realising that he liked to touch David's body, particularly that long appendage that was, as usual, rock hard. By the time they got into bed both of them were more than ready for some action. David started with lots of gentle kisses, gradually working his way down Gary's body. 69ing came next and David used that time to start opening up Gary's love tunnel. He was slow and gentle, only adding an extra finger when Gary was completely relaxed with what he had. David couldn't resist using his tongue as well so fingers and tongue fucking him soon had Gary wandering round in space. When he was sure Gary was relaxed enough, David used gel to lubricate them both before sliding his glans over a very relaxed sphincter. Slow penetration as he watched Gary's eyes. Still unfocussed, but David knew the boy was enjoying it, the sighs of contentment and the occasional little wriggle to make it more comfortable soon had David long stroking this new lover. He held on as long as he could and was rewarded by Gary having a mighty orgasm without touching himself. He had another one with David who thought he was going to black out, it was so intense. He fell forward, supporting his torso on his elbows and whispered in Gary's ear.

"That was wonderful Baby."

Gary pulled David's head down and planted a very intense kiss on his lips before replying.

"Thank you David, that was incredible. Will you stay in me and do that again?"

David was ecstatic, this boy that he had been attracted to the second he saw him was going to be ok with anal sex. He sighed with relief because he thought he might have kept him even if the anal had not worked.

They only stopped fucking when Gary said he was getting sore. They were both firing blanks by then, but the amount of cum on Gary's torso was testament to his enjoyment of the action.

"Come along my messy lover, time to shower and sleep."

# Part 3

Gary rolled onto his back, stretched, yawned and opened his eyes. The bed was empty and he knew it was late, the sun was shining and it looked incredibly bright reflecting, as it was, off the snow. He squirmed and thought he ought to get up. That thought coincided with the bedroom door opening and David walking in dressed in riding clothes.

"Ah, my sleeping beauty is awake. Time you showered, or we'll be so late for lunch it will be dinner."

He was laughing and Gary was happy.

It wasn't that late, just turned eleven when he emerged from the shower to find David now dressed in casual trousers, shirt and sweater.

"There's an estate polo for you Gary and I've borrowed a pair of trousers from Archer for you until your new wardrobe arrives."

He didn't really need socks with his canvas shoes but David produced them so he wore them. He was pleased to be dressing normaly now, the coveralls were ok but they defined him in a way he didn't like.

"No regrets about last night?"

Gary grinned. "Well, I'm not sure, I think you ought to fuck me several more times tonight for me to make a more reasoned decision."

David laughed until he fell onto the bed, spluttering, "I might be able to arrange that."

The house staff very quickly realised that the master had a new lover. Sighs of relief greeted that knowledge, David was so much nicer when he had a lover.

The field hands very quickly swamped Gary with affection, he had persuaded David to channel some heat into their quarters. The pinched look disappeared from their faces and David realised he was getting more work out of them.

"I think maybe I'd better milk you for more ideas about how I can more efficiently use my labour force."

Of course this all happened several weeks after their first love in. Gary was soon relaxed and confident enough with David's love to exert his normal character. He watched, he listened and he learnt. He saw a lot that David and the estate manager missed because they were too on top of it. The weather improved and Gary learnt to ride. He was soon joining David almost every day riding round the estate where he would see things that needed doing or changing.

During these first weeks, David started to fall in love with his new prisoner. Gary was doing the same. David lavished so much affection on him he was almost swamped, and even pleaded with David to ease off a little.

"I'm beginning to love you David, please don't smother me."

David laughed, "Ok, I promise. In fact tonight I think I might let you fuck Archer. I would like to choreograph a sex session between you two boys. Archer will be fine until you penetrate him but he knows it is going to happen occasionally."

Gary blushed.

"I know I will like that David, Archer and I are friends and he is very sexy, but do I have to fuck him, I know he hates it."

"Afraid so, I have to make him pay a little for his life of ease now. An occasional fuck beats working in the fields and I'll let him take you as well if you are friends."

Gary nodded but as soon as David retired to his office after lunch, Gary sought out Archer to tell him.

"David is going to choreograph sex between us tonight. I'm sorry, he says I have to fuck you."

Archer looked a little sad as he replied, "It's ok Gary, I knew it would happen sometime. I will try to make it good for you."

Gary leant in and kissed Archer on the cheek.

"I like you so much, I will try to make it good for you as well."

"I like receiving blowjobs so if you get the chance to do that I'll be happy."

Gary grinned, "No problem, I really like sucking cock so I bet I will like giving you one because I like you so much as well."

Archer was pleased, he just hoped Gary didn't have a cock as big as David.

\* \* \*

The evening turned out very much as Archer had expected. David was quite inventive and definitely hands on when choreographing everything. It started with Archer and Gary on the bed giving each other blowjobs. David walked round them stroking their bodies particularly their butts. He slid a couple of fingers in to Archer, well lubricated before replacing them with a butt plug, similar thickness to Gary's penis. Archer came off Gary to look at what David was doing because this was a new twist.

David sniggered. "I thought you might enjoy Gary's cock more if you were well opened up first."

Archer went back to sucking Gary until Gary said he was about to cum.

"We'll be nice to him tonight Gary, don't cum in his mouth, save it for his arse."

Archer was pleased with that. He didn't mind cum but he would sooner not have to take a full load.

"Up on your knees now Archer, legs spread wide, drop your shoulders on to the bed and use your hands to spread your anus. Gary, remove the butt plug and see how wide you can open him up."

Gary almost came on the spot. The butt plug had opened Archer up nicely so that his hands spreading himself further made his hole open quite wide.

"I don't think I will hurt him David even if I go in straight away."

"Ok, Lover, go for it."

Gary lubed himself and Archer before positioning and then easing over Archer's sphincter. He kept still until he felt Archer relax and then he completed the penetration. It felt wonderful, he started to slow fuck him with long strokes, watching his cock slide in and out of Archer's arse was an amazing sight, it was so sexy that he came much too quickly. After all the stimulation of Archer's mouth it wasn't surprising.

"Damn it Gary, you came way too quickly, I hardly had time to enjoy that."

"I'm sorry, David, Archer stimulated me too much with the blowjob, and I do like him a lot."

"Never mind, roll him over and get him an erection, then I'm going to let him fuck you. I want you to make love to Gary, Archer, but you are to do it permanently embedded in his arse."

Now that was something new. When Archer was erect, he lubed them both and slid into Gary in the missionary position. The feeling made him tear up. He had never fucked anyone before, and Gary was very sexy and his insides were amazing.

"Oh crikey, Gary, that feels incredible." He leant forward then and started kissing all over Gary's face and upper torso. "I think I could revise my sexuality if I was always a top and you were my bottom boy."

Gary smiled and whispered, "I think I might like that."

David was watching this and could see how much both boys were enjoying the loving, it gave him pause for thought. Perhaps he wouldn't use Archer again. The boys patently liked each other very much.

To finish this little orgy David fucked Archer as well and then made Archer watch him make love to Gary.

"Shower together and then you can toddle off to your quarters Archer."

David told Gary his decision after Archer had gone.

"I know you both enjoyed that little session my love, but as you and Archer are such good friends I won't involve him in our sex play again, except possibly at my orgies."

Gary was surprised, but pleased.

"Thank you, David, I'm sure Archer and I are going to become very good friends and I don't want to have sex with my best friend, even if he were gay."

David was surprised, he thought he saw something to make him jealous.

"Why ever not, I could see you enjoyed it all tonight."

Gary laughed, "Oh yes, I enjoyed it as well, but I think I would have enjoyed it with anyone. You have made me realise how much I enjoy gay sex. It was that extra bit special because I like Archer so much."

"Would you have sex with him in private if I allowed it?"

Gary wasn't stupid, he realised David was fishing because he was jealous.

"Oh no David, I love you now, you are so exciting to be with and you are so good to me. I would only ever have sex with someone else if you were there and sanctioned it. I am beginning to realise that sex, is just sex. It's very exciting but it isn't love, that is what you have shown me, and that is what is important to me now."

For David, that was the perfect answer. He would probably still involve Gary in orgies with friends, but what they had developing was special, and yes, he did love this boy. He would love him now without the sex.

"I am so pleased. I can still have my little orgies then because it is only sex."

"Your friends won't hurt me David, will they, and you won't let them do anything horrible to me, will you?"

David took Gary in his arms.

"No my love, we don't get very kinky. You may have to take a spanking on your bottom if you don't please one of my friends, but they are never destructive. Sometimes they just give you a tingle and make your next orgasm amazing. We always have enemas and showers so even if you have to rim someone it will only be the same as it is with me."

"I doubt that, you are special, I will enjoy it because I love sex, but not the same as doing it to someone I love."

Gary was saying all the right things to make David so happy.

David's love for Gary just kept growing, so his handling of him changed. He started to educate him into his ways. He taught him about good food and wine. Gary learnt to order from menus written in French and Italian. He could handle the array of cutlery and glasses at a tables set for fine dining. Because Gary sat a saddle so well, David started teaching him show routines for things like dressage, he also learnt to jump so that he could ride out with the hounds and not have problems with the fences. The GPS collar came off and his wardrobe grew to reflect his activities.

The very last thing that Gary expected from his new life was, effectively, a stepson. When David's son was born, Gary was nearly always there when David went to see him, and as he grew he came to recognise Daddy and Gary. Gary loved it. The boy, Andrew, was a lively little tyke, always wanting to be with the men instead of his mother.

"What are you going to tell him about me when he is old enough?"

"The truth of course, my son will not grow up with any prejudice. I have asked uncle to send me a few dark skinned prisoners. I want Andrew to understand that black men are just like us, it is only their skin that is different, the same will apply to homosexuals and lesbians. I want a well-balanced son ready to take over this title and estate when I die."

Their love life just kept getting better. Gary loved what David did to him in bed, it was incredibly exciting and satisfying. When David was feeling passive, making love to him was equally as exciting. He loved to be the top, and looking down on David, now beautifully tanned all over, made the orgasms amazing.

The orgies when they happened were fun as well, after he had gotten used to them. They didn't happen very often and David's friends were all attractive, well-educated Scottish gentry. Young, like David they were gay and bi-sexual. Gary had met some of them socially with their wives and ceased to be surprised when they would let him fuck them, as well as the reverse. The first one was a surprise and when a young black prisoner was included, that was also a surprise.

One afternoon when David was in Edinburgh on business, Gary sat in the library and let his mind wander back to that first orgy and the run up to it.

* * *

David came into their suite after riding that morning and after his shower he sat with Gary, took his hands, looking him in the eyes and told him.

"I have a few friends coming this evening to have dinner and play cards. We play for sex and I supply the boys that are going to be used for our pleasure. Tonight it will be you and Archer. I will be there all the time, but you can expect to have loads of sex with my friends, and maybe an exhibition fuck with Archer. I don't expect it to get heavy, my love, but you must always be enthusiastic and answer questions the way you think the guys want them. For instance, if one of them accuses you of not trying, or being a poor fuck and asks you what he should do, you must say something like, 'I am sorry, Sir, that I displeased you, please punish me for my lack of effort.' ok?"

David was smiling, and Gary thought, *'how bad can it get?'*, lots of sex, and maybe the chance to fuck Archer again, he would like that.

"Alright, David, I'll try not to let you down."

Gary had never seen the room they went to after dinner. They had gone back to David's suite first and Gary had douched before showering again and dressing in just a pair of very sexy shorts. No one else was there so Gary had a good look round. In the centre was a circular card table with six chairs round it, so, that was how many he had to deal with, he thought. Off to the sides were what looked like a weight bench, only a little higher, and with restraints fitted. There was a doctor's examination table with stirrups fitted, a table with some not so pleasant looking pieces of equipment, chatisers, dildos, butt plugs and gags, plus several bottles of Wet Light, and a bed, well more like a matress raised from the floor, but no headboard or foot board.

David saw where Gary's eyes went and laughed.

"Don't worry, they won't hurt you, you might get a red bottom but they won't bruise you, and you might be opened up bigger than normal, they do like to inspect your insides before filling them with their own cocks."

Archer entered then not looking very happy.

"Come along Archer, if you look like that when my guests arrive you will be nursing a red bottom in the morning."

Archer tried to look enthusiastic and achieved it when Gary gave him a hug and whispered. "You will probably get the chance to see my arse reamed out by lots of cocks tonight."

Both boys laughed and David looked pleased.

David told the boys they were to keep the guests glasses full with whatever they wanted and showed them the small bar that swivelled out from the wall.

Hamish showed the guests in a few minutes later.

Gary and Archer quickly scoped them out. They were all dressed very casually in jeans giving the boys a chance to assess their groin areas. They both gulped at Alexander when he was introduced. He was the smallest but his groin showed a substantial bulge, and that was, presumably soft. Iain and Braden didn't look small either, but the other two wore looser fitting trousers and very quickly showed that they were going to be voyeurs rather than participants.

The first two hours they played seriously for money. That was the reason two of them came. They put up with the games after because of their friendship with David.

There was nothing sophisticated about the game that followed. Strip poker, stud or drawer, dealer's choice. Gary or Archer would be asked to remove the article of clothing from the loser of each game and to make it as erotic as possible. The only rule was that underpants had to come off last. When a player was naked, the winner of that game had to specify a forfeit. It could be anything but in defference to the two non involvers, the winners chose the boys to give them blowjobs. So Gary blew one and Archer the other when they eventually got naked. Both men congratulated the boys and then were allowed to put their pants back on. David was the winner of the game that saw Alexander naked and Gary was designated to finish the disrobe and then get Alex an erection. It was huge and Gary sat back on his haunches and just stared before looking appealingly at David who just laughed.

"You may well take that later my love, but you can help your case by fucking Alex now. Take him to bed and show him how good you are, but don't take too long."

The cock was amazing and Gary did it justice before moving on to the anus and opening it up, he was encouraged to rim it and was so pleased that Alex smelt clean and fresh. When he slid over Alex's sphincter in the missionery position he was very gentle but made Alex produce a gusher as he orgasmed himself.

"That was very good, Gary, I will be gentle with you when we reverse roles."

Gary looked at Archer who just shook his head. When he could talk again as the men returned to the card table, he whispered to Gary.

"If David asks me to take that I'm going back to the fields, that's a true monster."

The game continued and Archer had to perform next. Braden was the loser and Archer was delighted to fuck him to orgasm. He wondered why the players didn't fuck their friends instead of letting him and Gary do it. The cock was a good size, but David was longer so Archer wasn't too worried if he had to take it later.

The next one had Gary and Archer goggle eyed. Archer had to remove David's last article of clothing and Iain who had won elected to fuck David.

"Sorry David, I know we usually let the boys do it, but I've fancied your arse for ages so now I'm going to take it."

"No problem Iain, but when I get the chance I'm going to have Alex fuck you."

Gary and Archer hugged themselves that would be some sight, watching Alexander's monster ream out Iain's arse.

David couldn't hide his pleasure as Iain fucked him slowly. The man had a very adequate cock in both length and breadth. Gary thought he would like that one as well, not as long as David but definitely thicker.

With everyone naked now, there was no more pretence at cards. David made sure they all had full glasses and then he told Gary to use any of the equipment he liked and to fuck Archer to orgasm.

"I want you both to enjoy it Gary, but I want great entertainment value from it as well."

That was no problem for Gary, he really liked Archer and whispered to him.

"I'll be so gentle with you but I am going to see how many different positions I can get you in."

"Mmm, sounds interesting, and I'll try to remember them all in case I get the chance to do the same to you."

Both boys laughed which pleased David as they started. Gary took Archer to the bed first and pampered him before attacking his groin and moving to his anus for some serious rimming and tongue fucking. Archer loved it and soon started to space out having his arse and his cock and balls excited.

Gary thought the others would enjoy seeing Archer with a dildo protruding from his arse while he continued to pleasure him, so he picked a suitable one, not too big and lubricated it and Archer. He made Archer pull his own legs back and wide, looping his arms through them, then he fed him the dildo and fucked him gently with it while he sucked and played with his cock and balls. He positioned himself so that the others could see everything and kept playing until he could see Archer losing it. Then he lubed his cock, eased the dildo out of Archer and replaced it with his own cock which he used to the best of his ability with long slow strokes while he continued to play with Archer's cock and balls. The action was perfectly timed and both boys came at once in gut wrenching orgasms. They were grinning like idiots as the six men applauded them.

"Ok boys, well done. Now go and clean yourselves and when you come back we'll have some more fun with you."

Archer and Gary gave each other douches and chatted.

"I wonder if I will really have to take Alex. He has got a monster hasn't he?"

Archer nodded. "I don't think I could," grinning, he continued, "But I would seriously enjoy watching him fuck you."

"Mmm, well I'd probably enjoy being an exhibitionist if he does fuck me."

When they got back to the play room they were surprised to see Iain being fucked by Braden. It looked very erotic, and Gary thought he would like to be in Iain's place. Braden was a very sexy man. When they finished, David took Gary to the table with the stirrups fitted.

"Up you get my love. I'm going to get you comfortable and then we are going to watch Alex perform."

Gary pleased David by grinning and saying very quietly, "When he has finished, I won't even feel any of the rest of you if you enter me."

Iain and Braden came back in and David got things moving again.

"Alright Alex, he is all yours, you can do what you like to him."

Alex grinned at Gary, "Well, I suppose the first thing I am going to do is paddle his arse for fucking me, then I'm going to cut him a new arsehole."

Gary didn't like the sound of that, and Alex appeared to be more aggressive than he had been at first.

He started by winding the stirrups further back and wider.

"You can all stroke his arse now and then feel it again after I have finished punishment, you'll be able to feel the increase in temperature, no problem."

With that, Alex went to the table to select his chastiser. He came back with a riding crop, which made Gary cringe in fear. He knew that would hurt monstrously no matter how soft Alex was. Alex laughed then and went back to the table, returning with a punishment paddle. The others all had a stroke of Gary's arse before positioning to watch.

Alex delivered ten, he spread them from halfway up the thighs to the top of the arse. Not too hard, but the three on the back of the legs really hurt, the seven to the arse started erotic but the last one was very painful. Then came the dildos. Each one he took got him applause from the others. The last one was almost as big as Alex and hurt going in because Alex didn't stop after insertion until Gary had it all.

"Now if you ask me very nicely, I will feed you the real thing, but I'll be very gentle with you."

"Please, Alex, will you feed me your enormous penis, it is such an amazing piece of equipment I will try to make it feel very welcome in my little bottom."

Everybody cheered and David moved in to give him a very passionate kiss.

Well lubricated, Alex positioned himself at the end of the table and moved in slowly until the head of his cock was resting against Gary's anus.

"Relax Baby and push down."

Gary tried, and he was pleased that the pain of entry was bearable.

"Thank you, Alex, you can keep going now."

It was a magical sight. Alex's monster slowly disappeared inside Gary before Alex pulled it out again, leaving just the head inside Gary's arse, then he went in again and continued the same procedure for a few minutes. Gary thought it was fantastic and voiced his approval. Alex then ceased being Mr. Nice Guy, instead he started pulling out completely, waiting for Gary's anus to close up completely and then plunging back in. He did it a few times, which made for fantastic voyeurism before David stopped it.

"Good sex is enjoyable sex for both parties, Alex."

David didn't need to say any more, Alex then fucked Gary to a terrific orgasm for both of them.

Cleaning up again and then Gary and Archer were subjected to a fuck fest round robin. On the bed alongside each other but in changing positions, David, Braden and Iain spent a few minutes fucking one of the boys before moving on. With one of them out of it for a few minutes and calming down, it took them a long time to orgasm, by which time the boys were getting sore. When it was completed, David sent them for showers and to get dressed. Back in the playroom, dressed properly, David addressed the company.

"These boys have done us proud, I think they should join us for Brandies in the library."

* * *

The next day, Archer and Gary were able to compare thoughts on the orgy.

"I could have done without the paddle and the first bit of Alex's fucking, but I thought the remainder was fantastic. I loved being able to fuck Alex as well."

"Yeah, I enjoyed fucking Braden and playing with you was great, but I hated all the fucking. I guess I really am a good heterosexual boy."

David was full of praise for both boys at breakfast.

"You can take the day off today Archer, as my thank you for being so good last night. Gary, my suite after you finish."

He sounded serious, Gary looked at Archer and just shrugged.

David was still thinking about the previous night making him very horny, so when Gary walked into the suite, David just said, "Strip, and then doggy fashion on the bed."

Gary got the quickest fuck ever then.

"Sorry Lover, I was just so horny thinking about last night."

Gary laughed, "I'm so pleased, I didn't want to let you down."

"You didn't my love, everybody was thrilled, and Alex apologised for getting carried away."

Gary didn't say anything, but Alex did hurt him when he pushed straight in after letting his anus close up.

# Part 4

David disturbed Gary's reverie calling him for lunch.

"What have you been doing this morning?"

"Reading mostly, but I also thought about our first orgy and how much I enjoyed it apart from Alex when he was pulling all the way out, that hurt."

"Yes, I told him about that, and as you know he hasn't done that again."

"No, but I wonder, David, does taking Alex make me less exciting for you when you fuck me?"

David sniggered, "No my Love, you are young enough and so fit that your sphincter soon closes up again after Alex has finished. Do you like him fucking you?"

Gary's turn to snigger, "Yes, well, he is huge and none of my insides can escape that monster when he rages around inside me."

"What about something even bigger?"

Gary looked at David with more than a little surprise on his face.

"You mean there is anyone bigger than Alex?"

"Mmm, he arrived this morning. I inspected him immediately and measured him erect, thicker and longer than Alex. Want to see him?"

Gary struggled not to sound too eager. He couldn't imagine something bigger than Alex, but he thought he would like to try it. How marvellous being reamed out by an even larger cock.

"Of course, particularly if you intend that I should take him."

"Would you like to try him?"

Gary laughed, "I don't know, I would like to see it first."

"Ok then, after lunch I'll call him to our suite and let you play, then you can decide if you want to try to take him. I'll be honest, I would love to watch him fuck you. I would probably want to follow on and orgasm forever inside you, it would be so exciting."

Gary was surprised to be confronted with a black man despite David saying he was going to ask his uncle for a black prisoner. The man looked to be about the same age as Gary and he was quite good looking.

He was wearing overalls and obviously freeballing because Gary could see the snake down his left leg.

"Martin has been informed, the same as you were, Gary, that if he performs satisfactorily as a sex toy he will remain in the house. If he doesn't he will be out in the grounds, not too bad now, but in the winter he will be a very unhappy bunny. You are going to perform for us aren't you Martin?"

Martin looked a little apprehensive but nodded his agreement.

"Gary is going to do some exploring of your body for a little while. Whatever he asks you to do I want you to do it without hesitation."

Again Martin nodded, so far so good, but the young man was obviously a little frightened.

"Hello, Martin, I'm another one of His Lordship's sex toys, and he wants me to see you with an erection because if I am very brave, he wants me to let you fuck me."

Martin's eyes became even wider with surprise.

"Now, will you take your overalls off and go to lie down on the bed on your back."

Gary gulped as Martin's cock was revealed, still flaccid. On the bed with the monster sat between his legs it looked even more impressive. Gary sat alongside him and started to fondle the flaccid cock, but it didn't stay that way for long. Within a few seconds Gary was confronted with a monster like nothing he had ever seen before. He thought Alex's cock was too big to be real, but this one defied description almost. First assessment was that it was definitely as thick as a coke can, so, about nine inches round. He lifted it to the vertical to assess it looking from the top, definitely longer than a foot, but by how much he wasn't sure. He looked at David.

"A shade under fourteen inches and a little under nine inches round."

Gary gulped, stroked the cock a few times, played with the balls as well before saying anything.

"Martin that is without doubt a stupendous piece of man meat and the thought of letting you plant that inside my arse is both exciting and frightening."

Martin smiled then for the first time.

"I would be very gentle with you if you wanted to try it."

Gary laughed then, "You would have to be or I would probably scream down the walls of this house. Have you had much experience of fucking?"

Martin shook his head, "Not much, a couple of girls took it and one guy, but I didn't know how to do it properly with a guy so I split him, but I'm sure I could do much better now because I know about stretching and lubrication."

Gary shuddered, looked at David and said.

"I would probably die if he went in dry, but if you want him to try me David, I'll let him."

David moved in and stroked Gary's cheek.

"Thank you my love, you know I would love to watch him."

"I know, and because I love you so much I'll try to take him."

"Alright, why don't you finish your exploration of him and then both of you go to Gary's bathroom, douche thoroughly and shower and then you can go turnabout fucking each other."

Gary didn't need asking twice. He continued to stroke Martin's cock and play with the balls for a few minutes before asking him to turn over and spread his legs wide, up on his knees. Gary stroked the cheeks for a few minutes, sliding between the legs to play with the perineum and balls as well before stretching the cheeks further to uncover fully a very tasty looking anus.

"Oh, David, I will have no problem lodging my little Gary in there, it is perfect."

David nodded, "Yes it is. Just slick up a finger and feel the insides, very soft."

Gary did, and couldn't resist finger fucking Martin for a little while.

"Mmm, very nice, let's go for our showers, Martin, I want to play for ages and let you try me."

David grinned, he had got used to Gary being a bit of a cock hound, but he wasn't worried because the boy never showed any interest in doing anything without him being there as well.

Mutual douches out of the way, the boys pampered each other, and Martin was full of questions. Gary told him the whole story, and how much better his life had been here because he loved man on man sex.

"I'm not suggesting that you will be able to take my place, but if you ask Archer he will tell you that even though he doesn't like gay sex he puts up with it because it gives him a good life here."

"I'll be ok, Gary, I was fucked a lot by bigger boys as I grew up in a gang and I don't mind it. I don't think I'm gay, but probably bi. I would prefer a girl but boys are fun and my arse is pretty flexible."

Both boys laughed and finished their ablutions.

Back with David, both naked, David scoped them out.

"Very attractive. Now Martin, I want you to take Gary to bed, play with him, make love to his body. You can go 69 when you want to start opening him up and when you think he is ready I want you to fuck him, flat on his stomach to start, I think, then doggy and finally missionary."

Gary thought that would be best as well.

"Gary, I'm going to record this because I think you should see it all and when you are on your front you will miss it."

"Ooh, lovely, we'll be able to watch the action as often as we like without me getting my arse reamed out, except by you of course."

Much laughter and Gary spread out on the bed, looked at Martin and spoke, "Ok, Tiger, take me to Paradise."

Gary thought Martin was a cute guy, he was very unsure of himself as he started pleasuring Gary, made worse because David was wandering round looking at the action. He soon got into it though because Gary's body was so small it was almost like making love to a girl to start with. By the time he got to the groin he was well into his stride and took Gary's cock into his mouth without hesitation. By the time they were 69ing, Gary was having problems, Martin's cock was just enormous. He licked it base to tip and down the underside taking in the balls. It was certainly exciting, but he began to worry about taking it in his arse. Alex was enormous and had hurt going over the sphincter, but Martin was probably another two inches round. All thoughts of that problem went out of his head when he felt Martin's fingers inside him. They were amazing, they didn't just move in and out. When they were inside him they moved around, particularly the first two because he could bend them, which he did, feeling all round Gary's inside.

"Oh God, Martin, I don't know what you are doing but please don't stop."

Gary giggled then and told David that he thought Martin's fingers were fully articulated. When Martin got to all five digits on one hand he tried to spread them. That was so sensuous that Gary had a massive orgasm. Martin drank it all down then turned Gary over and smacked his bottom, hard enough to make him squirm, but David noticed he was positioning ready to fuck and had the lube to hand. After about ten or twelve slaps, he lubed his cock and Gary's arse and positioned it so that a small push would have him inside. He leant forward and nibbled Gary's ear before making the entry. He only went in a couple of inches but Gary gasped in shock and then squealed.

"Oh fuck, that feels like a tree trunk."

Martin tried not to go in any more for a while and just nuzzled Gary's neck and ear whispering words to make him relax. It was a good ten minutes before Martin was lying against Gary's body pushing him into the mattress, with his cock fully embedded. He started humping gently then until he had Gary so turned on that he started pushing back as Martin thrust forward until he was in the doggy position making enough noise to wake the dead, he was so turned on.

"Oh yes, Martin, fuck me deeper, fuck me harder."

David was amazed how turned on his lover was but didn't stop filming it from every angle.

When Martin made Gary turn over they could see that he had already cum several times but was still as hard as a rock.

"Pull your legs up and wide, put your arms through them and keep them back."

Gary complied and then nearly hit the roof as Martin slid all the way in, deeper than he had ever gone. Gary screamed and came again as Martin upped the pace and joined him in a mighty orgasm. He took Gary's legs then and moved them to a more comfortable position as he continued fucking him gently until his cock was too soft to go back in, then he slid down alongside him panting but telling him what a fantastic fuck he had been. David put the camera down then and slid onto the bed alongside Gary to kiss him and get into position to fuck him.

"Sorry Baby, I have to do this."

Gary smiled and pulled David down to give him a very passionate kiss. Martin just looked on in surprise. That was probably the quickest orgasm David ever had. He had been so turned on watching that massive appendage moving in and out of his lover.

All sated and showered, David asked Gary what he felt about the last hour.

"I can't even begin to describe what it felt like having Martin inside me. It is just so huge that I don't think anything else, ever, will reach the parts of my body that his cock reached."

David looked at the flaccid cock of this new boy and then blushed a little as he replied.

"I might try that myself then, it certainly looked amazing as he used it on you."

Both Martin and Gary looked at David in wonder.

"Would you really let him fuck you David?"

"Mmm, I might."

Gary laughed, "Oh good, will you give me a blowjob at the same time?"

Much laughter and then Gary spoke again.

"I'm not up for it yet David, but can I make love to Martin some time. I'm sure it would be fun watching that monster become a fountain when I'm fucking him."

"Oh yes, definitely, I'll record that one as well. Now, let's go down and see what chef can rustle up for us, I'm quite hungry after watching you two."

Martin was wondering what he had got himself into. He was quite happy with what had just happened, Gary was, after all, a very sexy and cute guy. He thought that working in the house would be good as well, he had done plenty of manual labour but working outside in the winter didn't appeal to him. David cleared that one up over a snack.

"If you would like to carry on having sex occasionally Martin, I think we can accommodate you as household staff. I'll arrange for my maintenance manager to start teaching you how to look after all the household equipment, and the infrastructure of the house. Would you like that?"

"Oh yes please, Sir that sounds good."

"Well consider it done, as long as you behave yourself."

Martin grinned and assured David he would be very good, particularly in bed. The other two both laughed.

David was so turned on by Martin's huge appendage, even when soft that he briefed the tailor to make shorts for him that showed the appendage to best effect, and then instructed Martin that he was to go commando all the time in the house. That soon had to change though because the shorts always had dirt marks where Gary and Archer played every time they saw Martin during the day. Even when he was back to wearing his briefs he still looked amazing. David couldn't resist him either and took him for blowjobs several times a day.

The two big ones didn't take long to happen either. The first was David letting Martin fuck him while Gary recorded it, and also took part in the spit roast. The second one was an exhibition fuck for his card playing friends when Martin made love to Gary again, only this time they tried for as many different positions as possible. It was so erotic that both boys were fucked several times after their exhibition.

Nothing much changed then until Gary's five years was completed, then he and David started travelling, not spending too much time away because David didn't like to be away from his son for too long.

Archer and Martin had both finished their sentences and been released, given a helping hand by David, and behaving themselves to make sure they weren't seen in court again.

Gary kept in touch with both of them and David was pleased to be able to have a few more romps with Martin until he got married and settled down. Archer, of course never indulged in gay sex again.

David never took another permanent lover, but he and Gary continued to have outside sex with the prisoners until David's uncle retired from the bench and the supply stopped.

Andrew assumed responsibility for the estate when he was twenty-one leaving David and Gary to enjoy full time retirement.


## The End


Here is a sample from another story you may enjoy:

# DEXTER CHASE

# RUIN

## GAY HARDCORE

He came to my life when mum remarried after dad died. I was an only child that's why I was happy to have an older brother. He was very nice to me back then. I remember during that time, I was so convinced he's the big brother I've always wanted.

I have no idea why he changed and I can't tell you exactly when he became so. He used to look after me when our parents were away, which was frequent. He even chose the local college after graduation so that he could still live at home. He was being the best big brother in the world.

I was sixteen when he went to college and I think it was soon after that he started getting antsy with me for virtually no reason. I was devastated the first time he actually hit me. Dom was the jock, I was the nerd. He was the big guy while I was not exactly wimpy, but not a jock either. I wondered why he changed and once I knew it was permanent, I just avoided him as much as possible. He knocked me around a little almost every time he saw me, if our parents weren't around. It made me sad at first then I got resentful and confronted him.

"Why are you doing this Dom? All my life you've been my protector. You've looked after me. Now, it appears you get your satisfaction by bruising me."

He looked daggers at me then said, "Because," and that was it.

I guess I was Mr. Average. I was an average student academically. I didn't piss off the physical training staff, so I suppose I performed adequately there. I played all of the sports, but not well enough to make me qualify in any of the school teams. I had a reasonable number of friends and had no personal problems until I was about fourteen. It was then that I realized everyone else was talking about girls, dating, and having sex. I didn't like girls, so when I thought about having sex with them, it was merely like having mutual jack off sessions with friends. At that stage in my life, I was no one in particular. I was just another guy with a dick and balls. I had a few intimate sessions with my best friend, Jody. But I never touched his organ nor did I allow him to touch mine.

By the time I was sixteen, I knew I was gay. How did this brilliant boy reach that conclusion? Well, through gay porn sites in my laptop of course.

The need to understand my feelings was the trigger. I went to straight porn sites and watched guys doing it with girls. It made me want to throw up. Next, I tried gay porn sites. My reaction came out naturally. Watching guys sucking and humping each other had me so hard it was painful, and my orgasms were mind-bending when I masturbated over them. It was soon after that I noticed Jody didn't want to talk about girls too. Except, like me, to keep up with the conversation among our classmates. When we were alone, our topic would either be about sport stars or the young actors in Hollywood. We always watched sports programs and it was the runners that held our attention the most, with the swimmers coming in a close second. We both admired the swimmers' bodies but it was the runners, particularly black ones that had us glued to the screen. Those huge black dicks swinging around as they ran had us drooling, trying not to let each other see how turned on we were.

Call us slow if you like, but it was ages before either of us realized that we were both gay. We acknowledged the fact to each other when we were seventeen, but still, we didn't do anything about it. My eighteenth birthday was the big day. Jody told me he was going to give me a present that would blow my mind.

My birthday was on a mid-week so it was decided that I would have a party on the following weekend. On the actual day, Jody came home with me from school and we went straight to my bedroom.

"I'm going to give you your birthday present now, but for me to do that you will have to do everything I tell you," he said.

This was interesting so I gave him a quizzical look and he grinned at me.

If you enjoyed this sample, look for **RUIN**.

**Also by this Author:**

## From the Author

If you enjoyed any of my books then please share the love and click like on my books in Amazon.

If you write me a review and send me an email I will send you a free book, or many.
(Just know that these emails are filtered by my publisher.)

Good news is always welcome.

One Last Thing, For Kindle Readers...

When you turn the page, Kindle will give you the opportunity to rate this book and share your thoughts on Facebook and Twitter. If you enjoyed my writings, would you please take a few seconds to let your friends know about it? Because... when they enjoy they will be grateful to you and so will I.

Thank You!

**Dexter Chase**
dexter_chase@awesomeauthors.org

www.ingramcontent.com/pod-product-compliance
Lightning Source LLC
Chambersburg PA
CBHW071351130626
46556CB00005B/2133